If Sophie

Distributed to Schools and libraries
in the United States by
ENCYCLOPAEDIA BRITANNICA EDUCATIONAL CORP
310 South Michigan Ave.
Chicago, Illinois 60604

ISBN 089565-760-0
Library of Congress Cataloging-in-Publication Data
available upon request

If

Sophie

author: Anne-Marie Chapouton
illustrator: Pascale Meert

The Child's World
Mankato, Minnesota

If Sophie

hadn't wanted

a few carrots

to eat she wouldn't have

gone into

the vegetable patch.

If Sophie

hadn't gone into

the vegetable patch

she wouldn't have

left her basket there.

If Sophie

hadn't gone back

to the vegetable patch,

she wouldn't have fallen

down in the lettuce.

If Sophie

hadn't

fallen down

in the lettuce,

she wouldn't

have lost

her handkerchief.

If Sophie

hadn't lost

her handkerchief,

Sebastian Broom
wouldn't have
found it.

And,

if Sebastian Broom

hadn't found

Sophie's handkerchief

in the vegetable patch,

he would never

have dared

to follow Sophie

to give it

back to her.

If Sebastian Broom

hadn't dared

follow Sophie

to give her handkerchief back,

he wouldn't have
seen her going
into the woods.

If he hadn't

seen her going

into the woods,

he wouldn't

have seen

Fangs the Wolf

following her.

And, if he hadn't seen
Fangs the Wolf following her,
Sebastian Broom wouldn't have
knocked Fangs the Wolf flat with a
good punch in the stomach.

And, if Sebastian Broom

hadn't knocked Fangs the Wolf

flat with a punch in the stomach,

Sophie wouldn't have looked back.

So,

if Sophie

hadn't felt

like eating a few carrots,

and hadn't gone to the vegetable patch,

and hadn't forgotten her basket there,

and hadn't gone back again,

and hadn't fallen down in the lettuce patch,

and hadn't lost her handkerchief...

And,

if Sebastian Broom hadn't found it,

and hadn't dared to follow Sophie,

and if he hadn't seen her

go into the woods,

and if he hadn't seen Fangs the Wolf,

and if he hadn't knocked him flat

with a good punch in the stomach…

Sophie wouldn't
have fainted away
in his arms.

And,

Sophie would never,

never, never have dared

hug Sebastian Broom!

THE CHILD'S WORLD LIBRARY

THE LOVE AFFAIR OF MR. DING AND MRS. DONG

LULU AND THE ARTIST

THE MAGIC SHOES

THE NEXT BALCONY DOWN

OLD MR. BENNET'S CARROTS

THE RANGER SMOKES TOO MUCH

RIVER AT RISK

SCATTERBRAIN SAM

THE TALE OF THE KITE

TIM TIDIES UP

TOMORROW WILL BE A NICE DAY

THE TREE POACHERS